JASON AND THE GOLDEN COIN

MONIKA ROSSA WHEATLEY

Kravitz & Sons
INNOVATORS IN PUBLISHING, MARKETING AND ADVERTISING

Kravitz and Sons LLC
204 E Arlington Blvd. Suite B
Greenville, NC 27858

Published by Kravitz and Sons LLC.
ISBN: 979-8-89639-566-9 (sc)
ISBN: 979-8-89639-567-6 (e)

Jason's birthday party lasted only two hours, but it was very pleasant. All the invited guests showed up—friends and family—and, of course, everyone brought a present for the birthday boy. After all, to be eight years old is serious business and people seemed to know that. So when it came time to open the presents, Jason was very excited.

He pulled out all of the games, electronics, trucks and cars, a super-soaker, and lots of other things. But when he opened the last bag and pulled out an old and very worn-out teddy bear, everyone became quiet. Jason looked around and saw his elderly auntie smiling at him and nodding her head. He simply couldn't thank her. It was clear to everybody, including the auntie, how disappointed he was.

...and saw his very old auntie smiling at him and nodding her head.

"Boring and cheap," he muttered under his breath, not really caring if anybody heard him. Jason put the teddy bear back inside the bag, and didn't look at it anymore.

That evening seemed like all the other evenings. Jason had soup for dinner and, after taking a bath, he was ready to go to bed.

When his mom came in to read him a story, Jason was already very tired. The story was interesting, and Mom knew how to read a story to make it seem almost real. His sleepiness went away. When Mom tucked him in and turned the lights off, Jason's eyes were still open.

At first, in the darkness of night, he couldn't see anything. Only the moon outside the window. "Looks like a coin," he thought, and turned his head away.

And then...he saw it: a shiny little object right under his desk, close to the wall, between the cracks in the wooden floor. Jason turned on the light to see. He got up from his bed and crawled under the desk. The door opened. It was Mom.

"Jason," she said, curious. "What are you doing under your desk?? Aren't you sleepy?" She sounded worried.

"Oh." Jason was a little confused. "Nothing, Mom. Really … nothing. I am going to bed."

After Jason's mom left the room, he looked at the shiny object. "Tomorrow," he thought, "Tomorrow I will get a screwdriver or a knife from the kitchen. And I will dig that thing out." And then he fell asleep.

The next evening during dinner Jason asked if he could use a knife to spread the butter on his piece of bread. Mom was surprised.

"Jason," she said, "you never wanted to use a knife before. Maybe you are a big boy now and you want to eat like adults. Here it is," she said. And she pulled a butter knife from the drawer. Somehow, when they were cleaning up the table, nobody noticed that Jason put the knife into his pocket. He took it to his bedroom and hid it in a shoe by his bed.

And she pulled a butter knife

from the drawer

When Mom came in to read the story, Jason was already sitting on his bed in his pajamas.

"Can we do something else tonight?" he asked.

"Like what? I guess you don't want me to read you a story. So, what do you want to do?" she asked.

"I would like you to tell me a story," said Jason quickly. "I would like to hear the story of this house."

Mom looked at Jason and smiled. "There is really no story to it. I grew up in this house. That is all there is to it. This …," and she spread her arms around, "… used to be my room."

For a moment there was silence.

"There is nothing … nothing more you can tell me?" Jason was disappointed.

"Not really. It depends what you are looking for, what you want to know."

Jason thought about the shiny object but didn't say anything.

Jason's mom kissed him goodnight, turned off the lights, and closed the door. Jason waited a little bit longer to get up than on the previous night. Only after he heard his parents talking in the kitchen, noisily doing the dishes, did he jump out of bed. He turned on his little flashlight. He took the knife out of his shoe and crawled under his desk. There, working with the utmost care, he finally pulled the shiny object from between the cracks.

he finally pulled out the shiny object

It was a coin. A golden coin. A coin like Jason had never seen before.

"Thank you for taking me out of that dark place." Jason heard a man's voice and it scared him.

"Don't be silly!" the voice laughed. "It is me. What are you afraid of?"

Suddenly Jason could see what was happening. The man on the coin was talking to him!

"Who are you?" asked Jason, as he carefully put the coin on the night table.

"Don't you know?" The voice now seemed surprised. "Hmm … actually, I guess you wouldn't know. Well, my little boy, I am the Czar. Or, I should say, I am a portrait of the Czar. I am just one of very many portraits."

"The Czar?" asked Jason. "This is the first time I have ever heard about such a thing. What or who is a Czar, and what does it do?"

"A Czar
is a King.
Or maybe
even more
than a king."

"A Czar is a king. Or maybe even more than a king. Certainly more than a president," was the answer.

"How can that be? I thought that the president is the most powerful person. At least that is what Dad says."

"Well, imagine," said the Czar, "the people of your country have to choose your president, but people don't choose a Czar. The Czar is born a Czar. Isn't that great?"

Jason wasn't convinced, but it really didn't matter at this point.

"Where did you come from?" asked Jason.

The Czar laughed.

"My little boy," he said, "I wouldn't even know where to start my story. What do you really want to know—how I was made? In the mint, my boy, in the mint."

Jason didn't know what a mint was. When he heard "mint" he thought of chewing gum or candy, but it turned out that a mint is the factory where money is made.

"For example, the coin that bears me is a five-ruble coin," said the Czar.

Jason had never heard of rubles but the Czar quickly explained to him that rubles were just like dollars, but were money from a different country.

"I used to be worth a whole big horse!"

"I used to be

worth

a whole

big horse!"

"Oh! How this could be possible?" Jason was very surprised.

"Very simple, my boy. Very simple. Somebody bought a horse using me, I mean, my coin. The horse was bought for five rubles, and this coin that carries me is a five-ruble coin, as I said."

"You mean that somebody exchanged a Czar for a horse?" asked Jason.

"You silly boy," the Czar chuckled. "You can't trade a Czar for a horse, but at one time, a long time ago, you could exchange a five-ruble coin for a horse. What an idea!" said the Czar, as the eyes in his face rolled.

Jason thought for a while, and then he asked, "So could I buy a horse today, paying with you?"

"I don't think so," said the Czar. "You see, the worth of a coin changes with time. Sometimes its value goes up and sometimes it goes down."

This idea was too difficult for Jason to understand. But he was more curious about the Czar. "Where did you come from and how did you come to be on this coin? What else happened to you?" he asked.

The Czar smiled. "It might seem that it is fun to be on a coin. Everybody wants you. You represent something. You represent the value of things that people want to have. So yes, once I was used to pay for the horse, for a piece of land, for a loaf of bread, for a new dress, for school tuition, or for …," the Czar rolled his eyes again. "I can't even list all of the things I was used to pay for."

Jason was thinking hard. "For a loaf of bread? How can it be that a horse could be worth the same as a loaf of bread? Compare a horse with a loaf of bread. The same coin paid for both the horse and a loaf of bread?" Jason was very surprised.

The Czar nodded his head. "I told you. The value of the coin changes at different times. I was used to pay for a loaf of bread during a revolution, when things were scarce. The lady who had me at that time was hungry. Her children were hungry, too. She went to her neighbor who was a baker and asked him if he could lend her two loaves of bread. She said that she would pay him later, when times would be better and she could find work."

"And?" Jason was curious.

"The baker wouldn't wait. He wanted his money right away, and even more money than the bread was normally worth. Everybody in the village was hungry. It was a difficult time to get food. Remember? Revolution."

"What is a revolution?" Jason didn't hesitate to ask.

He wanted

his money

right away

The Czar sighed slightly. "Revolution is like a war. It is more like civil war, actually. And you know what war is, don't you? Anyway, it is war, but people say that war, or a revolution, has a purpose. What war or a revolution does, though, is it makes people hungry and angry. Coins like me might not buy a horse anymore, but a simple loaf of bread or two. Tell me, aren't you tired? Are you sure you don't want to sleep now?" asked the Czar.

Jason quickly sat up on his bed. "Oh, no, no, no! I am very interested. I mean, it is very interesting, all those stories. Tell me, what happened later?"

"That all depends what you think 'later' means," the Czar said, "but to make the story short: I ended up inside a curtain rod, right above a window, in a city taken by war."

"Curtain rod?" repeated Jason.

"Yes, the one that holds the curtains in the window, you know …"

"Oh," Jason understood. "How did you end up in there?"

"I was pushed in," the Czar said, "along with a lot of the other coins. They were just like me, pushed in one against another. We were hiding."

"What do you mean, hiding?" asked Jason.

"Well, our owner at the time hid us there. And guess who the owner was?"

Jason had no idea.

"I guess I will surprise you. Your Granny Lucy."

Now Jason was almost speechless. "Granny Lucy! My great-great-grandma! How do you know about her? I only saw her in my mom's picture album. But you? Are you sure we are talking about the same person, my mom's grandma? Granny Lucy?"

The Czar smiled. "Yes, yes, yes," he said. "You know. It was wartime. We were Granny Lucy's wealth. We heard the sounds of battle all the time. Eventually, the enemy's soldiers walked into our city, and Granny Lucy with her family had to leave and run away. So they did. But before they left the city Granny Lucy took us out of the curtain rod. She cut a small hole in her little son's jacket, and simply sewed us into the lining. What do you think about that?" The Czar was smiling.

"Tell me,
what
happened
next?"

Jason was very surprised.

"Ha, ha, ha, ha." The Czar was very amused. "My boy, of course I know who used to own me! I know how I happened to find myself in the crack in the floor here in this room, too! Guess what? It was really your Granny Lucy's doing."

Now Jason decided that he would focus on the story only, without unnecessary questions. "Okay," he said, "just tell me the rest of the story."

"I told you that your Granny Lucy had sewn me, along with other coins, inside her son's jacket. We had to leave the city really quickly since the enemy's army moved forward very fast. We walked out early in the morning. Granny Lucy carried her little boy when his legs got tired. I still remember the warmth of her hand that passed through the fabric of the little boy's coat on my golden face as she carried us. An older sister of the boy, your Nana Hanna, walked all the time by herself. On her way to the unknown, Granny Lucy was paying with other coins for bread and lodging. After a long journey she finally found a place to stay in a little village where the war—as she thought—couldn't reach them. She lived in a small room with her two children, waiting for your Pappy, her husband, to come back from the war.

"One day, when her little son was playing in a sandbox with other children, she heard him cry out. She rushed outside, and she saw him running to the house with one side of his little jacket completely ripped out. The golden coins were falling out while he was running!"

Jason was speechless. Now his eyes looked like two coins themselves.

She cut a big
hole in her
little son's
jacket, and
simply sewed
us into its
lining.

"Your great uncle—he was Nana Hanna's little boy—was having a fight over a bucket. Somebody had pushed him, and an old nail sticking out of the sandbox bench ripped out a side of his jacket. The golden coins fell out, and the children in the sandbox started to pick them up, forgetting about the bucket and the fight."

"...and the children in the sandbox started to pick them up."

For a while the Czar and Jason were quiet. Both of them were thinking about the story. In his mind the Czar saw how it happened, and Jason imagined it in his.

"Granny Lucy picked me up from the ground. She picked up three of us golden coins altogether," the Czar said.

"Who did?" asked Jason.

"I already told you—Granny Lucy. Who else do you think?!" said the Czar, a bit annoyed.

"Ah …," said Jason, "… and?"

"She took us to the house and put us into a special box. She said she would save us for emergencies."

"Do you know what those emergencies were?" asked Jason. He re-ally wanted to get to the end of the story and find out how the coin ended up on the floor in his room.

"My little boy," the Czar smiled, "of course I know. Granny Lucy didn't need to use us to pay for things, or emergencies, anymore. We three coins were sewn into her daughter's wedding dress for good luck. Her daughter was your Nana Hanna, your mom's grandma."

"...I was put in your grandma's shoe when she was marrying your grandpa."

"Whose wedding dress?" Jason was lost.

"Your Nana Hanna's wedding dress. And it became a tradition. Your great-grandma, in turn, put one coin in the wedding dresses of each of her daughters. She had three daughters. In fact, you know one of them. Your Old Auntie was one of them," the Czar added, hoping that adding Old Auntie would make it easier for Jason to understand. But it didn't. For Jason, Granny Lucy got mixed with Nana Hanna, and also sometimes somebody had three coins, and sometimes just one. It didn't make any sense. He started to feel tired.

"Did you at least bring any luck to this bride, whoever she was?" Jason asked.

"I am not sure," said the Czar, "but you know what? You can ask your mom. The last time I was supposed to bring luck to someone, I was stuck in your grandma's shoe when she was marrying your grandpa. Hmm … I don't know if I brought her luck." The Czar was silent for a moment.

"What happened then?" asked Jason.

"I will tell you, but my boy, it is a secret. You may never have known about this story if I didn't tell you. But I am telling you so you will know how different the fate of any coin can be…and also, maybe …" But here, the Czar didn't finish.

"Here it is," he finally said. "I was given to your mom."

"To my mom!" cried Jason. "You are actually my mom's coin! She never showed you to me! She never told me anything!" Jason could barely sit still. He was very excited. He was waiting for the next part of the story.

The Czar was silent. His wrinkled forehead showed that he was deep in thought.

"Come on!" insisted Jason. "Now you have to tell me everything I want to know. Are you really my mom's coin?"

"Okay, okay," said the Czar. "I will tell you. But you have to remember one thing: nobody knows—well, I want to say, your mom never knew how special I am. Nobody told her."

"You mean you never talked to her?" asked Jason.

"Never. There was never an occasion."

"How did my mom get you?" Jason couldn't wait.

"I was her graduation present," answered the Czar.

"A what?" Jason was surprised again.

"I am telling you. When your mom graduated from high school, your grandma Emily was very proud of her. At that time the family didn't have lots of money, and therefore your grandma Emily couldn't afford to buy an expensive graduation present. But she was very proud of her daughter, and she wanted to celebrate in a special way. So, guess what? She took me out, a golden coin, and gave me to your mom!"

Jason and the Czar sat quietly for a while.

"And that's it?" Jason finally asked.

" *I was her graduation present*"

"No, of course not."

"Then tell me, what happened next?"

"Well," said the Czar, "it might sound very awkward or unbelievable to you, but when your grandma Emily gave me to your mom, your mom laughed at me. She snorted sarcastically, 'I didn't know that nowadays teenagers get golden coins as presents. I thought they get an iPod, or a gift certificate, or really something better than that old coin!' Your mom then threw me up into the air. She looked for me later, but not for too long. She just didn't care …"

The room was quiet. After a while, Jason's gentle sobs could be heard.

"Why was my mom so mean?" he asked.

"She was not mean. She just didn't care. She wanted an iPod, that's all. And many years later she really regretted throwing me away," said the Czar.

"How do you know? Did she tell anybody?" asked Jason.

"No, but over the years she looked for me many times. And see, I had my ways of keeping out of sight, in between the cracks of the floor. I didn't want her to find me. I wanted YOU to find me. That's why I made myself shiny a couple of days ago. I knew you would see me in the moonlight."

"Why did you want ME to find you?" asked Jason.

"It is very simple. There are two reasons to it. First of all—and this is very important to remember—if somebody gives you a present, no matter how big or small, you should be grateful and happy. You should never say, 'Oh, how boring and cheap, this is ugly, why didn't you get me something better than that...' You don't know how much it took for the person to actually come up with the present, what the giver's intentions were ..."

"She snorted sarcastically. Then she threw me up into the air."

Jason's cheeks became red, but the Czar couldn't see them in the dark and Jason was grateful. He remembered the birthday party, and the stuffed animal that his old aunt had given him. He also remembered her saying that it was a very special toy. He remembered himself saying out loud, "Couldn't I get something better? This teddy bear is old and worn out."

The Czar gave Jason a little time to think, and then he said: "The second thing is that sometimes in life, when time goes by, it can be too late to say, 'I am sorry,' or, 'I didn't understand.' We should never let that happen."

"What are you talking about?" said Jason.

The Czar yawned. "Ask your mom tomorrow. You can show her what you have found. Now let's go to sleep. It is very late."

Saying that, the Czar turned his head to the side and his silhouette froze in place, and the coin looked again just like a normal coin.

"...it can be too late to say

I am sorry"

The next morning Mom had a very hard time waking Jason up. He seemed so groggy that she finally asked, "Are you all right this morning?"

Jason finally showed up in the kitchen, still in his pajamas. At first, he didn't say anything. He sat by the table and stared blankly at his bowl of cereal. He opened his fist showing his palm to his mother. In the middle of his palm was the golden coin.

In the middle

of his palm

was the

golden coin.

"Wow! Jason!" His mom was very, very surprised. "Where did you find it? I looked for that coin for years!!"

"Why did you look for it?" asked Jason.

"Why?" she cried, "Oh, Jason, because I lost it. I lost it a long time ago. Where did you find it?"

"Between the cracks of the boards in the floor, in my room," he said.

"Well, well, well." Mom's eyes became very shiny. Jason could tell that she was looking for something far, far away in her memory. "In a crack in the floor of your room, hmm …" She seemed like she was daydreaming.

"What is strange about that?" asked Jason.

"Jason," Mom said, looking a little sad, "it is a long story. Maybe I will tell you someday. Now, eat your cereal. You will be late for school."

And Mom started to mop the floor.

The next day in the late afternoon Jason was in his room doing homework. His mom was cooking dinner, and the whole house smelled like fried onions and tomatoes. "Spaghetti!" thought Jason, and he smiled. Mom's spaghetti was always very good. At first when the phone rang, Jason didn't pay much attention. But after a while Jason realized that Mom was talking to his Old Auntie, the one who had given him the old teddy bear for his birthday.

"Auntie," Mom was saying, "I hope it is not serious. We will see, hmmm, after all the blood work is done. You will be able to calm down. Please don't worry and don't miss any doctor appointments. If you need a ride, or if you need anything, please call me. I will come and help you."

Jason didn't fully understand what made him go to the kitchen. He certainly hadn't planned to. To his mom's amazement, Jason asked for the telephone receiver. Mom gave it to him.

"Auntie? Good evening, Auntie," he said, "this is Jason."

"Jason, sweetheart,
how are you doing?"

"Jason, sweetheart, how are you doing?" said the familiar voice on the other end of the line.

Jason heard himself clearing his throat. "I am doing very well, Auntie, thank you," he said. "How about yourself?"

"Oh, baby, old age is not much fun. But I am alright, I am alright," she repeated.

"Auntie, listen, please," said Jason, "I wanted to thank you for the teddy bear that you gave me for my birthday. I would like to apologize for what I said when I got it as a present from you."

"Honey, I understand. Thank you, you don't have to apologize."

"I do. I do have to tell you that I am sorry. I wasn't thinking. I really like this teddy bear. I think it wants to tell me something …"

"Oh, yes, it is a very special teddy bear. Maybe on Sunday I could stop by and we could chat. Would that be all right?"

"Sure it would, Auntie. I will wait until Sunday. Have a good evening, Auntie," said Jason, and he gave his mom back the receiver.

Mom stopped doing the dishes, came close to Jason, and gave him a warm hug. "It was so nice and thoughtful of you to talk to Auntie. What made you change your mind?"

"I just thought I should," said Jason.

"I am so proud of you. See, honey, I never …" She paused with that glazed look in her eyes.

"Never what, Mom?" asked Jason.

Mom's face was close to his and he could see that she was crying. "Nothing, nothing, it is too late now. You see, Grandma Emily died a long time ago. But I am so happy that you said that to Auntie, Jason." And she hugged him again.

Jason looked at the kitchen table. The coin was still there just as he had left it in the morning. For a moment, Jason thought that he saw the Czar's face smiling. But when he moved closer Jason saw that he was mistaken.

"Just a golden coin," he thought.